TESTIMO

Gwyneth Jones: "Well done, Janet, a book more than overdue. *Eve* was a delight; your sequel *Sarah*, about the rise of Abraham from Sarah's viewpoint, gave a hint of her tenacity and inner strength."

Jane Karman: "*Sarah: Emerging from the Shadows*, Janet Boast's sequel to *Eve*, is an evocative treatment of the rise of the House of Abraham, a most welcome addition to my collection of biblical stories. My young girls are just approaching their teenage years and the story is well within their grasp. I can most certainly recommend the book."

Ivor Godwin: "I had the pleasure of reading an advance copy of Janet Boast's *Eve: Biblical Women Emerging from the Shadows*. I found the unusual viewpoint relating to biblical stories well worth reading. A gentle fable about the condition of women rarely given any prominence in day-to-day religious instruction."

Biblical Women

Deborah

Emerging
from the Shadows

JANET BOAST

Published by Janet Boast Books.

Printed in the UK.

To contact the author/publisher regarding bulk discount pricing, etc, email janetboastbooks@gmail.com – or visit www.janetboastbooks.com

Special thanks for artistic contributions:
All illustrations by Katerina Mashlyatina.
Cover and book design by Ken Leeder.

FOREWORD

Following on from Janet Boast's series about the lives of the women who established Abraham's line, she now brings us *Deborah: Emerging from the Shadows*, set in the period of Israel's early history.

While the culture and worldview may be very different from our own, there is a timeless quality to the characters' hopes and fears, joys and griefs, and their quest to reconcile their understanding of God with the struggles of physical life.

Janet gives us a fable expressing reverence and joy for the spiritual nature that underlies the physical reality of human life.

DEDICATION

This story book is dedicated to everyone who opens it.

My thanks go to all those who inspired me to take up a notebook and jot down word plays that had simmered in my mind for some time.

This book was inspired by my own meditation and through the workshops presented by my dear friend Heather, which brought out my creativity.

My equally dear friends Jo, who owns the Chingford Bookshop, and all the girls who go to her Tuesday evening get-togethers – Lisa; Eileen and Dave, her husband; and Julie, Jo's sister; as well as Tracy, Luciana and Jackie – all said "Go ahead!"

Last, but not least, thanks to my dear friend Nicholas, and to Christopher John Payne and his team at Effort-Free Media (Doreen Martens, Farah Deogracias, Naomi Munts and Ken Leeder) who helped Nicholas to get this book into print.

All of these are true friends, and I thank them for opening my heart up to Yahweh's loving care.

ABOUT THIS BOOK

Woven into the fabric of the work are elements drawn from the universal human experience and the environment in which we live.

The Bible predominantly deals with the affairs of men in the presence of Yahweh (God): kings, prophets, the victorious and vanquished, the rise and fall of empires. But it has very little to say about women, who after all gave birth to the men.

This book has no pretence to scholarship, biblical or otherwise, but rather reflects possible insights into the fortitude of women in biblical times.

Deborah

Jeshua was a judge who lived in a small village in Ramah with his wife, Marian. He gave advice to the villagers when they had a problem.

The two of them longed to start a family, but Marian didn't conceive, so they prayed to God. They promised that, if God granted them their wish, they would dedicate the child to God.

God heard their plea and, a few months later, to their delight, Marian found she was pregnant.

When Marian gave birth to a little girl, they named her Deborah. When she was six days old, they took her to the priests to dedicate her to God.

They were told to bring her back when she was six years old. During those six years, Marian gave birth to two sons: Joshua and Ehud.

When Deborah turned six, her parents took her back to the temple.

Deborah was told that she would have to leave the family to serve God. She was very sad to go because she loved her family. She cried as they left.

One of the priests said, "Don't cry, child. You will see your family from time to time," and that made her feel much better.

They decided that she would live with the head priest as part of his family, as they didn't have a girl, only boys.

She went to be taught with her "brothers," as she called them, and knew she was lucky because girls didn't usually get an education.

She learned how to read the scriptures, how to write, and all about the Israelite nation and how their faithfulness to God shaped their lives. She loved God with all her heart.

As Deborah grew up, she set all the boys' hearts aflutter, for she became a tall, beautiful woman, with unusual chestnut hair and hazel eyes that always seemed to smile.

It was her nature to care for people. She loved to help them, and they went to her for advice. She always told them to listen to God, because He loved them so much.

The priests and elders got together and decided that God wanted Deborah to be a judge. So she became the youngest judge the Israelites had ever had.

She took her seat under a palm tree between Ramah and Beth-El in the highlands of Mount Ephraim. The people took to calling it "Deborah's tree." She sat outside so all the people could listen to her judgments.

Deborah always judged wisely, and all the people loved her. Whenever she was holding court, people flocked to listen to her.

She met her husband, Lappidoth, at one of her meetings. He was a kind, gentle, loving man who loved God as much as she did. He helped her as much as he could with her work, and she often asked his advice. He joked that he was not only married to Deborah but also to the whole of Israel, and he was very, very proud of her.

The Israelites were living under the rule of Jabin, king of Canaan, who had his court in Hazor. He respected Deborah and often asked her questions about her God.

The captain of his army, Sisera, hated the Israelite people and dealt very harshly with them. He often clashed with Deborah over her judgments, and he hated her having the king's ear.

They had been under Jabin's rule for more than 20 years.

The people came to Deborah and said, "We're sorry we have displeased God. Please can you ask God to help us? We hate being treated as slaves by Sisera.

"He has a thousand chariots now, and he uses them to trample our lands, ruin our crops, and uproot our vineyards. We sometimes don't have enough food for our families, and children are dying."

Deborah said, "I will speak to God on your behalf, but you must give up your false gods and go back to living as God wants you to." The people promised they would and started praying in the temple again.

One day when Deborah was communing with God, He told her, "Deborah, I have listened to the people. I have heard their cries, and I will help them."

Deborah said, "What can I do, Lord? What can I do to help?"

God said, "Send a messenger to Barak, son of Abinoam, from Kadesh in Naphtali, and say, 'Please come to see me, as God has heard the voice of the people.'"

25

A few weeks later, Barak arrived. Deborah told him he was to assemble an army of ten thousand men from Naphtali and Zebulun. He was to arm them with the ox-goads a ploughman uses to prod his oxen, adding metal tips to them to make weapons.

Deborah said he should get food for the journey, and said, "You are to go to the top of Mount Tabor when I tell you the time is right."

Barak replied, "Deborah, we will not get to Mount Tabor without Sisera knowing. He has eyes everywhere."

Deborah said, "Leave that to God; He will have a plan. Just get the men together and get your weapons ready.

"I will let you know when to march. This is on the authority of God. He will not let his people down; he will set them free."

Barak said, "Deborah, I will not go unless you come with us. You have the ear of God. He can tell you the best day to attack."

She said, "I will talk to God. In the meantime, get everyone ready to move at a moment's notice."

God told Deborah, "Yes, go with him. Because he has doubted my word, he will not be the one to kill Sisera."

Deborah talked it over with her husband, and he said, "Of course you have to go. It is from God."

She sent a message to Barak, telling him she would go with God's blessing. "He has commanded I go with you."

A few months later she received word from Barak to say that every man was armed and ready to leave.

Deborah was summoned to the king's house, and when she arrived she was sent straight in to see him. She found Sisera was in attendance too.

Her heart sank. She thought that somehow Sisera had found out what they were up to. Silently, she prayed to God to help her answer well.

The king smiled at her and said, "I won't keep you a minute. I'm just seeing to Sisera. He has informed me that there is an uprising in the far end of my kingdom. It seems so big that he needs all his chariots and men. I told him to go straight away."

Sisera said, "Why did you tell that woman everything? It has nothing to do with her people. They are too timid to cause trouble."

This made the king angry. "Sisera, you are only the captain of my army. You can easily be replaced. Deborah is my friend, and I respect her judgment. So go and put down your rebellion, and don't come back until it is over."

The king said, "Deborah, I am sorry about Sisera – I don't think he likes women." Deborah smiled at the king and said, "I am used to his nastiness. I take no heed of it. What did you want to see me about?"

The king said, "I am puzzled about the judgment you gave the other day to the two vineyard keepers. How did you arrive at that answer? I would have been furious if I had been the one who lost, but they went off arm in arm."

Deborah smiled and explained to the king that the answer was easy. She had just pointed out that they had forgotten a point in their law that said they were to help one another.

The king said, "I still don't understand," so Deborah spent the next hour explaining the law by which her people lived.

As soon as she left the king, she sent word to Barak to say, "Hurry! I will meet you at the top of Mount Tabor."

Mount Tabor rose to 1,886 feet above the northeast section of the Jezreel Valley, and from it you could see for miles around. God had chosen well the place for the Israelites to fight, for halfway up the slope it was thickly wooded, and Sisera would not be able to use his chariots.

When Barak arrived with all the men, they quickly set up their tents and sat sharpening their weapons.

Deborah and Barak sat down, and Deborah told him about the plan of attack that God had told her.

She said, "When we see them coming across the valley, we will hide up in the trees, and in the dense forest, and in dugout shelters that we will cover with forest foliage. So get your men to start digging the shelters.

"Some of us will be at the forest edge, up in the trees, and when the army has passed us, we will climb down and kill the men left to guard the chariots, disable them, and then come back at the rear guard. So they will be surrounded on all sides."

Deborah said, "You will be with most of the men up here on the summit and will kill them as they appear, as they will not be able to form a proper line as they come through the trees. Then work your way down and meet the rest of our men and me."

Barak said, "Deborah, will you be fighting? Do you know how hard it is to fight? We men are used to battle."

Deborah said, "I was taught the art of warfare with the boys at my lessons, and I have my own weapon. Don't worry about me, Barak. I was taught well, and my weapon was my prize for mastering the lessons."

CR

They had been camped on top of Mount Tabor for a month, going through all their

training. Every man knew just where to go and what to do.

Word got to them that Sisera was back, and that he knew that they were camped on Mount Tabor and was getting his chariots ready. He would soon be on his way.

That night in camp was a sombre time; the men chatted in whispers, realising that by this time tomorrow some of them could be dead or injured.

Deborah, sensing the mood, told Barak to call all the men together. "I will talk to them. I have a message for them from God."

When they were all assembled, she said, "Don't be apprehensive about tomorrow. God has said He will be with you, and you will have a resounding victory. Let's give thanks and pray to God now, and know that you cannot fail, as God is with us. Tomorrow, Sisera and his army will be no more, and we as a people will be free."

So all the men bowed their heads and prayed, then gave a big cheer for Deborah and went cheerfully off to their beds, ready for the battle the next day.

In the morning, the men were up before dawn, ate their meal in silence, and got their weapons ready. As dawn was breaking, the lookout said he could see movement in the far distance.

Barak said, "This is it, men. It's time to free our people."

Deborah said, "Let's say a quick prayer to God and give thanks for our freedom from tyranny this day."

They all prayed, then quickly got into their positions. Some were going to the shelters, others climbing the trees and using the foliage to hide.

Deborah, with her group, moved down through the trees to the edge of the forest; each man knew which tree to climb.

Deborah waited until everyone was up in their tree, and she walked all around but couldn't see any of them. They had hidden well.

Pulling a rope that had been left dangling, she hoisted herself into her tree, and when she was settled she pulled up the line.

Deborah's tree was right on the very edge of the forest. She was sitting calmly, but her nerves were twitching. Then she heard the sound of a horse snorting and the jingle of bells that were attached to the reins.

She gave the signal to the men with her that the enemy was here. She peeped through the branches of her tree and moved her head back as Sisera's face came into view.

Grasping her weapon, she watched as more and more chariots appeared.

Sisera tried to carry on in his chariot, but the trees were too close together. He jumped off his chariot and signalled to all the other men to do the same.

He was almost standing under Deborah's tree; she found herself holding her breath.

Sisera barked orders, telling about a dozen of his men to stay with the chariots.

To his second-in-command, he said, "Let's go up through the trees and finish off these Israelites once and for all. Then I can tell the king that that woman Deborah organised the threat to his kingdom, and that will get her out of my hair permanently."

Signalling to his men, he set off confidently through the trees. Deborah signalled to the men hidden in the trees to climb down, as the army had passed all the trees they were hiding in.

Silently they climbed down, and Deborah then led them to attack the dozen men Sisera had left behind, who were so sure of victory that they hadn't bothered to set lookouts. In fact, they were all together, and some of them were playing a game.

Deborah's men surrounded them and, at her signal, rushed together towards Sisera's men. They were so surprised, they didn't put up much of a fight and were soon dispatched.

The men then unhitched the horses and sent them, with a smack on their rumps, down to the plains below. Then they pushed the chariots after the horses, and watched them smash on the rocks that were littered across the hillside.

Deborah said to her men, "Now we can return to the top to help Barak."

As they went through the trees, they could hear the fighting going on above them. Suddenly they could see men rushing back, and Deborah, with her sword raised up in front of her, rushed to meet them.

The sun came glinting through the trees and seemed to light up Deborah's hair. In an instant, the men who were fleeing saw this tall woman with what looked like flaming hair, brandishing a sword, rushing to meet them. They lost their nerve and were quickly overcome.

Sisera could not believe his whole army was being wiped out. He turned and fled, with the whole of the Israelite army at his back. Amid the noise of the battle and the cries of the wounded, he leapt down the mountain and ran for his life.

Heber, who was a Kenite, and his wife, Jael, had cut themselves off from their clan, the tribe of Kain. The clan was descended from the father-in-law of Moses, and they were nomads who had come into Canaan with Judah.

Heber wanted to settle down and to stay in one place. He was a friend of Jabin the king and knew Sisera well. He had pitched his tent under the oak of Zaanannim, not far from Kadesh, on the plains near Mount Tabor.

Sisera saw Heber's tent and rushed towards it.

Jael came out of the tent. She said, "I'm afraid Heber is not here at the moment. Can I do anything for you? Where are your chariots and your men?"

Sisera said, "They are on Mount Tabor. I still cannot believe that I have lost my army to the Israelites."

Jael said to Sisera, "Rest a while. I will give you something to drink, and you can sleep until Heber comes home. He will know what to do.

"If anyone comes to look for you, I will tell them that you and some of your men rushed by."

Sisera went into the tent and said, "I won't forget this kindness. You and Heber will be handsomely rewarded."

Jael said, "Hush now, you must be very tired. Sit here on our bed."

She warmed some goats' milk and said, "I will put some herbs into it to make you sleep. Nobody will bother you here."

After he had drunk the milk, she told him to lie down, and she covered him up. She sat on a stool outside the tent until she could hear him snoring.

She then went back inside the tent, took a tent peg and a mallet, and walked over to Sisera. Holding the tent peg against his forehead, she drove it into his temple using the mallet. She killed him instantly.

She then calmly sat outside her tent until Deborah and Barak turned up.

She took them into the tent and said simply, "He was a horrible man, and I have killed him."

Deborah hugged her and said, "God told me that he would be killed by a woman. You have carried out God's wishes."

The whole of Sisera's army was wiped out, and the people rose up and killed the king and all his people, so the land was at last free.

There was much singing and dancing. Songs were sung about Deborah, Barak and Jael; the celebrations went on for many days.

The people went to the high priest in the temple and asked him, on their behalf, to ask Deborah the Warrior Judge to rule over them.

The priest sent for Deborah to come to the temple. When she arrived with her husband, he told her what the people wanted.

She was shocked. "I don't know how to govern," she said. But the priest said, "The people want it, and you must do it. Only you can keep them loving God and following our laws."

She looked at her husband, and he took her into his arms and said, "Deborah, this is

what you were born for. This is what God wants you to do – to look after his people."

Deborah ruled the people with God's guidance, and with her husband by her side.

Barak was the head of the army, and he put down any insurgency that occurred.

Deborah was still saddened when people were killed, and she always dealt kindly with the prisoners they captured.

Deborah governed the people for more than 40 years and, in that time, there was peace.

She was known as the Prophetess, the Mother of Israel – the only judge ever to receive such a title – and when she died the whole nation mourned her.

And the song of Deborah is still sung to this day.

THE END

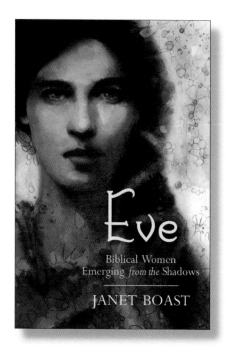

In time, Abel made an altar to Yahweh, and he gave the best of his flock as a sacrifice, thanking Yahweh for his love.

Cain saw what Abel had done and also decided to make an altar. On it, he put some wheat he had grown—but not the best, only the kind fit for animals. Yahweh thanked Abel for his offering, but said to Cain: "Am I not worthy of the best?"

This made Cain angry. He said to his father, "Why didn't Yahweh accept my offering, when he accepted Abel's?"

Adam said, "Who knows what's in Yahweh's mind. Don't let it worry you. Come, help me plow this new field."

Cain brooded all that afternoon, and when he saw Abel coming down from the hillside, his anger boiled over. Picking up a large rock, he waited for Abel to come closer. When Abel spoke to his brother,

One night, Eve lay in Adam's arms, as she did every night. But in the morning, when Adam awoke, she didn't stir. He looked at her peaceful face and knew she would never speak to him again.

He said a prayer to Yahweh for her safekeeping, then went out to tell the others. They buried Eve next to her beloved Abel, and Adam spent long hours sitting beside the

Several months later, Seth went to Adam and realized that he had gone to join his beloved Eve. They buried him beside his

Also available

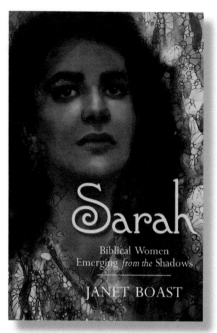

to see her privately, she said, "You have to do something. He wants to make me his queen! I just wish you hadn't lied to him."

Abram was alarmed when Sarai told him: "You have to tell him the truth, that I am your wife."

That night, Abram asked Yahweh for help. The next day he went to the palace, intending to speak to the pharaoh. He didn't know what would happen. He feared that he and Sarai would be cast into prison and maybe killed. So with a heavy heart he asked to see the pharaoh and Sarai.

He caught the pharaoh in a good mood. He told Abram, "Your sister will be my queen and you will be my brother." Then Sarai entered the room and he promised her, "You will have everything your heart desires."

Abraham was silent for a while. Sarai said, "Tell him!" Abram, looking at her, saw that she was afraid also.

The pharaoh said, "T...

ready. Suddenly she stopped when the story Isaac had just told her sank in.

"Isaac, say that again," she demanded.

"I was to be the sacrifice. Father put me on the altar and was sharpening his knife. Mother, I was so scared."

"I was lying on top of the wood that father and I had gathered. But it was alright, because Yahweh said, 'Abram, you have proved your loyalty to me.' And then we saw a lamb caught in a thicket, and father sacrificed it instead."

Sarai was so angry at this, she rush out of the tent, stormed up to Abram, smacked his face.

"How dare you put our son through an ordeal!" she cried. "I will never let yo my son away again!" The pent-up emoti the past few days suddenly erupted, collapsed into a flood of tears.

Abram gently picked Sarai u her into the tent, and told her the w "Yahweh was testing me, that's all never have let me sacrifice him."

Her emotions spent, Sarai it, Abram. I don't care what Y You are never to take my so

Also available

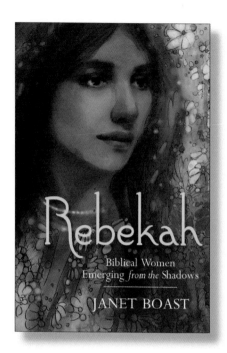

One day Rebekah went into Isaac's tent and said to him, "My beloved, you are getting old, so I think it's time for you to give the blessing to the firstborn."

"I guess you're right," Isaac replied. "Send Esau to me."

Esau was annoyed that his father had sent for him as he was just going off with his friends on a hunting trip. He was a morose boy with a fiery temper. Marching into the tent, he demanded, "What is now? I was just off on a hunt. Can't Jacob deal with it?"

Isaac said, "Son, your mother has reminded me that it is time to give you your blessing as the firstborn. As is the custom, I want you to find the finest young animal and make me a meal. You know the custom: you have to prepare it yourself."

Rebekah knew then that this was the man she had dreamt about. Shyly she smiled up at him.

"Is it much further to your camp?" she asked.

Together they walked into Abraham's camp, where he was waiting to greet her. As soon as Abraham saw her, he knew that God had picked the right girl for his beloved son.

That night the whole camp came to Isaac and Rebekah's wedding. There was much feasting and drinking of wine, singing and dancing. It was a joyous occasion.

When the time came for Isaac to take her to their tent, Rebekah was relaxed and happy. She knew the age gap didn't matter.

Rebekah walked over to her husband, full of love, and kissed him.

"I have never doubted your love for me, or for our boys. I think we have done as our loving God wanted. And Isaac, when Jacob comes to you for your blessing, tell him how much you love him. Tell him you forgive him for deceiving you. After all, he didn't want to do it. It was my idea."

With that, she walked out of the and went to get Jacob.

Also available

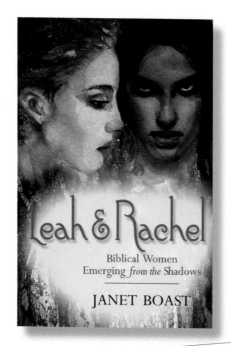

Leah & Rachel

Biblical Women
Emerging *from the* Shadows

JANET BOAST

LEAH AND RACHEL

As soon as Leah saw Rachel's lovely eyes and smiling face, she disliked her. Right away, she felt jealous of all the attention the baby was getting from her brothers and her mother and father.

EMERGING FROM THE SHADOWS

As the two girls were growing up, Leah began to hate her sister more and more. She was jealous, for Rachel was popular with everybody – always smiling, always willing to help everyone, even her sister.

Rachel was thrilled, as she had fallen in love with Jacob. But Rachel was still young, not quite sixteen.

Leah and three of her brothers were visiting their elder brother and his wife in the next camp, and didn't get back home till the next day.

Leah went to see a friend who worked with herbs and said, "I need a sleeping potion, and Rachel has asked for a potion to help her get pregnant quickly, so she and Jacob can start a family."

Her friend said, "So the wedding is going ahead then? I thought you were going to try to stop it."

Leah replied, "My father has found a husband for me, so I will leave here after my wedding and I won't have to see that sister of mine any more."

"I am glad for you and for Rachel," her friend said, handing her the herbs she wanted.

Laban put on a celebration for the wedding with much feasting, dancing and wine, and everybody

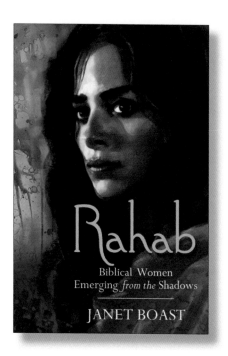

Some people were packing to leave; others were looking anxious. She didn't linger as she normally did. People just didn't want to talk. She got her provisions and went home.

She hadn't been home long when there was a knock on the door.

When she opened it, two strangers stood before her. One said, politely, "We heard that you have a room to rent, and we need a place to sleep for a couple of nights. Would it be possible for us to rent it?

She liked the look at them. "Yes, I have room. My last lodger went off this morning, so please come in."

She showed them the room and told them how much the rent would be. Smiling, they said, "We will pay you now," and gave her the money.

She told them the ~~provi~~

be ~~~~

When the two men were hidden, she went down and admitted the soldiers. They searched everywhere without finding her lodgers, and then told her she was to be taken to the king's chambers. "He wants to know about the two strangers you have taken in."

She was very frightened as the soldiers led her into the king's presence.

He looked at her and said, harshly, "Harlot, I want you to fetch those men to me for questioning. We can't find them anywhere."

Her knees shaking, she told him, "I did have two strangers stay, but they have left. They left through the gates before they were shut for the night.

They started walking around as usual. Then, suddenly, the man with the ram's horn started blowing it, and all the people started to shout and sing. The drums began beating and the trumpets bellowed. The noise w~~as~~ tremendous, and nobody in the city cou~~ld~~ hear themselves speak.

People put their hands over their ea~~rs~~ try to drown out the noise.

Then the city walls started shakin~~g~~ the soldiers, who were trying to put a~~~~ their bows, couldn't stay on their feet.~~~~

As the shaking became mor~~e~~ part of the walls began to break ~~~~ tremendous crash, the huge cedar ~~~~

The Israelites came rushing~~~~ opening, as more and more of t~~he~~ crashing down.

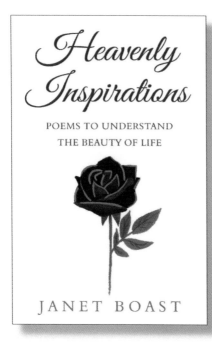

Janet Boast's poetry gives us insights in the quest to understand the beauty and complexity of the gift of life that is granted to all of us. Her poems help us to more deeply appreciate the importance of the creatures and lifeforms that God has bestowed on planet Earth to share with us.

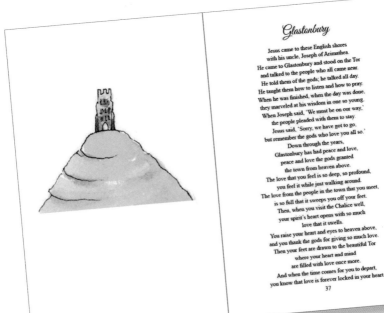

Glastonbury

Jesus came to these English shores
with his uncle, Joseph of Arimathea.
He came to Glastonbury and stood on the Tor
and talked to the people who all came near.
He told them of the gods; he talked all day.
He taught them how to listen and how to pray.
When he was finished, when the day was done,
they marveled at his wisdom in one so young.
When Joseph said, "We must be on our way,"
the people pleaded with them to stay.
Jesus said, 'Sorry, we have got to go,
but remember the gods who love you all so.'
Down through the years,
Glastonbury has had peace and love,
peace and love the gods granted
the town from heaven above.
The love that you feel is so deep, so profound,
you feel it while just walking around.
The love from the people in the town that you meet,
is so full that it sweeps you off your feet.
Then, when you visit the Chalice well,
your spirit's heart opens with so much
love that it swells.
You raise your heart and eyes to heaven above,
and you thank the gods for giving so much love.
Then your feet are drawn to the beautiful Tor
where your heart and mind
are filled with love once more.
And when the time comes for you to depart,
you know that love is forever locked in your heart.

37

Guardian Angels

We may believe that Angels live in heaven up above.
But that's not so, as they live here, with all of us.
They are with us through life, wherever we go,
through all of our lives, the highs and the lows.
They comfort us when we have a bad fright.
They dance with us when we have a joyful, fun night.
They are with us through our sorrow and our pain,
with us when honors by hard work are gained.
So if we go through life and make them our friends,
they will live and love us, right to the end.

Love

There is a God and Goddess
who gave us eyes to see
the beauty of a sunset, a rainbow,
and the blossoming of the trees.
There is a God and Goddess
who gave us ears to hear
a guitar, a piano, a choir
singing loud and clear.
There is a God and Goddess
who gave us a nose to smell
the scents of all the flowers
in the gardens, where they dwell.
There is a God and Goddess
who gave us lips that we might speak
of the love they gave to us,
and to everyone we meet.

It's a Puzzlement

What makes the clouds get so angry
That they go so very dark,
and then you hear the harsh sound of th
and see lightning, flashing sparks?
Why do they send us fearsome hurrican
that scour the land and knock dow
trees and other things?
And why do they make the sea so angry
and sends huge waves that rush i
so everything it spoils?
Then suddenly, the sky again turn
and it no longer seems like n
And the clouds have lost their a
and are again all soft, fluffy an

35204565R00044

Printed in Poland
by Amazon Fulfillment
Poland Sp. z o.o., Wrocław